Sadie and the Big Mountain

For Sadie and Ori with love —J.K.
For Don —J.F.

Copyright © 2012 by Jamie Korngold
Illustrations copyright © 2012 by Julie Fortenberry

Kar-Ben Publishing
A division of Lerner Publishing Group, Inc.
241 First Avenue North
Minneapolis, MN 55401 U.S.A.

Website address: www.karben.com

Library of Congress Cataloging-in-Publication Data

Korngold, Jamie S.
    Sadie and the big mountain / by Jamie Korngold ; illustrated by Julie Fortenberry.
        p.   cm.
    Summary: When her synagogue's nursery school plans a hike to celebrate Shavuot, the
holiday commemorating the day the Jewish people received the Ten Commandments, Sadie
is not sure she will be able to climb a huge mountain. Includes facts about the holiday and a
recipe for blintzes.
    ISBN 978-0-7613-6492-4 (lib. bdg. : alk. paper)
    [1. Shavuot—Fiction. 2. Ten commandments—Fiction. 3. Nursery schools—Fiction. 4. Jews—
United States—Fiction.] I. Fortenberry, Julie, 1956– ill.. II. Title.
PZ7.K83749Sac 2012
[E]—dc23   2011018797

Manufactured in the United States of America
1 – DP – 12/31/11

Sadie
and the Big Mountain

By Jamie Korngold

illustrated by Julie Fortenberry

KAR-BEN
PUBLISHING

Sadie loved school.

About Shavuot

Shavuot celebrates the time the Jewish people received the Torah. The holiday is celebrated seven weeks after Passover. The word Shavuot comes from sheva which means seven. Shavuot also marks the harvest of the first fruits of summer. Some say the words of the Torah are as sweet as milk and honey, so we eat dairy foods such as blintzes at the festive meals.

About the Author

Rabbi Jamie S. Korngold, who received ordination from the Hebrew Union College-Jewish Institute of Religion, is the founder and spiritual leader of the Adventure Rabbi Program. She has competed in marathons, national ski competitions, and rode her bike across the US at age 16. She has worked as a street musician in Japan and as a cook on a boat in Alaska. Rabbi Korngold is the author of *Sadie's Sukkah Breakfast* (Kar-Ben) *God in the Wilderness* (Doubleday), and *The God Upgrade* (Jewish Lights). She lives in Boulder, CO with her husband and two daughters.

About the Illustrator

Julie Fortenberry is an abstract painter and a children's book illustrator. She has a Master's Degree in Fine Arts from Hunter College. Her illustrations have appeared in Highlights High Five, Ladybug and Babybug Magazines, *Sadie's Sukkah Breakfast* (Kar-Ben) and *Pippa at the Parade* (Boyds Mills). She lives in Westchester County, NY.

Sadie knew she could reach the top of this Mt. Sinai, and together she and her classmates climbed to the very top, giggling and skipping all the way.

"Actually," explained the rabbi, "Mt. Sinai was not a very big mountain. It wasn't even the biggest mountain in the area. God chose a small mountain to teach us that anyone can climb high enough to reach God."

Rabbi Jamie took Sadie by the hand. "Come outside with me." She pointed across the playground to the mountain they would climb. It was the hill right behind the synagogue, where children played after Shabbat services. "There's our Mt. Sinai," she said.

"Why it isn't such a big mountain at all!" Sadie exclaimed. "Rabbi, that mountain's not big enough to be Mt. Sinai."

Rabbi Jamie saw how scared Sadie looked. She knelt down beside her and asked what was wrong.

"I don't think I can climb a mountain as big as the one Moses climbed," Sadie whispered.

"But Sadie," said Rabbi Jamie, "You're good at climbing. You have a walking stick to lean on. Your friends will be there to help you. And don't forget, we'll have blintzes to eat when we get to the top."

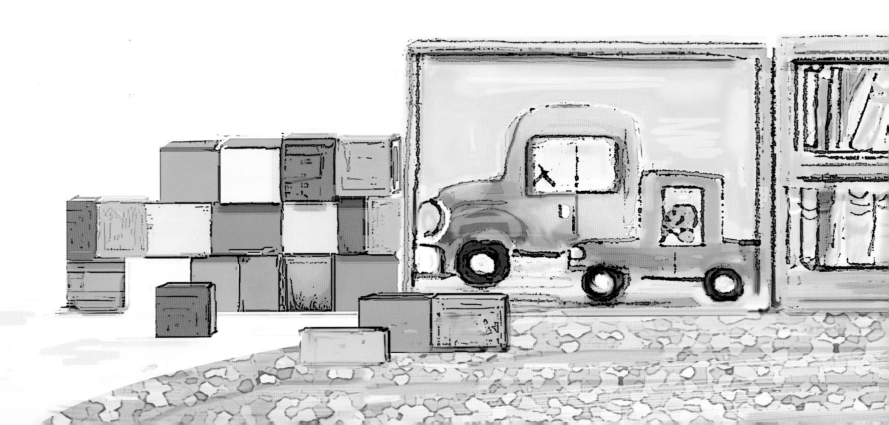

When Sadie arrived at school, Rabbi Jamie and Morah Sarah were waiting in the classroom to lead the children on the hike.

Everyone was wearing sturdy shoes, and carrying walking sticks. Everyone was excited. Everyone but Sadie. She stood apart from her friends and worried.

On Friday morning, Sadie woke up. She checked all over her body for spots. Nothing. She did not have chicken pox or poison ivy. She did not have a stomach ache or the flu. Sadie didn't even have a sniffle.

Anyway she was sure that by Friday she would have the flu.

On Thursday, the children made the batter and filling for the blintzes they would eat at the top of the mountain. As they stirred the eggs and cheese together, Sadie thought, "I love blintzes. But I don't think I can climb a mountain as big as the one Moses climbed."

"Does that mean the other boys and girls would help me if I have trouble climbing the mountain?" Sadie wondered. "I could never climb a mountain as big as the one Moses climbed. Anyway, I'm sure by Friday I'll have poison ivy."

1. I am the one and only God.
2. Do not pray to other gods.
3. Do not say bad words.
4. Celebrate Shabbat.
5. Love your mother and father.
6. Do not hurt anyone.
7. Married people should love each other.
8. Do not take anything without asking.
9. Do not tell lies.
10. Be happy with what you have.

On Wednesday, Morah Sarah explained that the Ten Commandments teach us how to get along with other people and God. "They tell us to not to steal or to lie, to listen to our parents, and to celebrate Shabbat," she said. "We need these rules to get along and to help each other."

Sadie decorated her walking stick with pink paint and red glitter. But she thought to herself, "I'm sure I won't need it. I could never climb a mountain as big as the one Moses climbed. Anyway, I'm sure by Friday I'll come down with chicken pox."

On Tuesday Morah Sarah taught the children how to make walking sticks.

"Moses carried a big staff, which helped him get to the top of the big mountain," she said. "The walking sticks will help us when we climb."

And there were never enough snacks.

Anyway, she was sure that by Friday
she would have a stomach ache.

All the children clapped with excitement.
All except Sadie. Sadie hated hiking.

Her hiking boots always hurt her feet.

Her backpack was always too heavy.

"This year," said Morah Sarah, "we will spend the week getting ready for Shavuot and then on Friday, Rabbi Jamie will lead us on a hike up our own Mt. Sinai."

"What a big mountain that must have been," thought Sadie, "to reach all the way up to God. I don't think I could ever climb a mountain that big."

One Monday morning at circle time, Morah Sarah said to the class, "Friday is Shavuot, the day the Jewish people received the Ten Commandments." She told them how Moses climbed all the way up to the top of Mt. Sinai. "When he came down forty days later, he was carrying two tablets with God's laws," she explained.

She loved the boys and girls in her class, and she especially loved her teacher, Morah Sarah.

She loved the Hebrew songs they sang during music, the tall climbing gym they played on outside, the feathery red hats in the dress-up corner, and the stacks of smooth wooden blocks on the toy shelf.